A Finder's Magic

A Finder's Magic

Philippa Pearce

illustrated by Helen Craig

CANDLEWICK PRESS

My mother wrote this story for her grandsons, Nat and Will. (The hero's full name is an anagram of the two of theirs put together.) She wrote it to be illustrated by their other grandmother, Helen Craig, but Philippa died no sooner than Helen had begun work. She would have loved the result: a book perfectly embracing so many of the people and things she held most dear.

Sally Christie

Dedicated to Nat and Will, of course

Helen Craig

Chapter 1
THROUGH THE GARDEN GATE

THERE WAS A BOY WHO WENT TO BED IN DESPAIR. All night he dreamed his despair, and he woke to desperation. Then he slept again and dreamed, this time a short, strange dream. He dreamed of a garden gate and someone waiting there.

He woke, and it was still very early. He dressed quickly and went out of the house to the garden gate. And there was someone, a stranger, waiting for him—an odd-looking little old man, hardly bigger than himself, and dressed all anyhow.

"So you got my message," said the old man.

"Yes," said the boy.

"Last night I was passing your house," said the old man, "and I looked in on your dreaming. It was very sad dreaming for a boy of your age."

The boy said nothing, but tears began to ooze from his eyes.

"'Losers weepers,'" said the old man. "I thought you might have lost something."

"Somebody," said the boy.

"I make no promises," said the old man, "but I might be able to help."

"I'd like that," said the boy. He cheered up a little. "By the way, my name's Tillawn, but everyone calls me Till for short."

"Till," said the old man. He didn't say what his own name was, and Till didn't ask. "Till," repeated the old man. He laughed creakily. "I'll keep that name in mind *till* I need it."

"What?" said Till.

"If you don't get it, you don't get it," said the old man. "Now, who've you lost, and how, and where? Tell me, because I'm a Finder—one of the old Seekers Finders. I could help you, if you'll also help yourself."

"I'll do anything," said Till.

"Then tell me," said Finder.

So Till began the story of how he had lost his dog, his frisky little dog named Bess. Every day, Till took his dog for a walk. First of all, she was on a leash, because he was taking her through the streets of the town where they lived. Beyond the town they came to a certain meadow called Gammers' Meadow. Here, Till let Bess off the leash to run free and play. After her playtime, Till put the leash on again. Then boy and dog went home together.

Yesterday Till and Bess had set off as usual, but in her eagerness, the little dog had pulled and pulled on her leash and twisted and twisted on her collar, until at last—

"The worst thing happened," said Till. "The metal ring that joined the collar to the leash twisted loose. Then she was free! She rushed ahead and was out of sight in a minute. I ran after her, calling and calling all the way, but when I reached the meadow—"

Till paused, remembering that breathless, desperate pursuit.

Finder said, "She wasn't in the meadow?"

"She wasn't there," said Till. "And it was all my fault. I knew the metal ring was worn. I knew she needed a new collar. I'd already bought her a really good one with my own money. It was in my pocket. I knew I had to change the collars. *The new one was in my pocket.*" He touched his pants pocket. "Still here. Useless."

Finder said, "You never know . . ."

Till said despairingly, "She wasn't in the meadow; she's not come home since; she might be anywhere. Lost . . . lost . . ."

"Lost," Finder said briskly. "Well, we certainly know where to start: we know where we are. Or, rather, where we should be: in this meadow you speak of."

"But she may have gotten lost on the way there," said Till.

"Just possible," said Finder, "and we shall not forget such a possibility. But I think that dog knew where she wanted to go, and she'd have gotten there. If so, the mystery we have to solve is why she wasn't still in the meadow by the time you arrived, what happened to her there, and where she went."

As he spoke, the old man was reaching with his left hand over the top of the garden gate to unlatch it from the inside. Till saw that on the first finger of his left hand he wore a ring of some dark metal, not gold, not silver; it wasn't a grand ring at all, and it was age-worn almost to a thread.

Finder said, "Pull the gate open, boy. Walk through."

Till set his hand on the top bar of the gate to pull it open,

and he felt a shock as though the gate itself had stung him. He snatched his hand back.

But, "Walk through," said Finder again. So Till tried a second time, and again the touch of the gate hurt him, so that he jumped back from it.

"The passage through can be tricky," said Finder. "Foreman shall help you." He laid the first finger of his left hand on the gatepost and held it there. Then, "Walk through," he said a third time. This time Till pulled the gate open without any hurt and walked straight through into . . .

Gammers' Meadow.

Chapter 2
OLD MISS GAMMER

"NICE PLACE," SAID FINDER, standing with Till in the middle of Gammers' Meadow and taking in the view. "Nice little flock of hens. Own henhouse, too. And what's that? Oh, a swing of sorts . . ." He had noticed the old car tire hanging by a rope from one of the tall trees that grew in the meadow. "And a river, too. Very nice. Nice for your dog, if she goes swimming."

"Never," said Till. "Unless she has to. She hates water."

Finder nodded. Then, looking around again: "You never said anything about people living here."

Two cottages stood side by side in a corner of the meadow, overlooking it. Till explained that the two Miss Gammers lived in them, one in each cottage. They owned the meadow.

"Sisters? Or cousins perhaps?"

Till supposed they were related in some way.

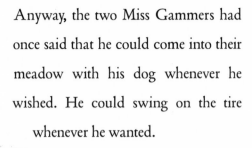

Anyway, the two Miss Gammers had once said that he could come into their meadow with his dog whenever he wished. He could swing on the tire whenever he wanted.

"Lucky boy," said Finder, but he spoke as if he were no longer thinking of Till on the swing. Instead, his gaze was fixed on the cottages. He said, "If either of those Miss Gammers had looked through a back window yesterday, she might—she just *might*—have seen your little dog here. She might have seen what became of her."

Till supposed so.

"You haven't asked either of them?"

"No."

"Why not?"

"The younger one—they're both old, but one's younger than the other—the younger Miss Gammer had just left home when I knocked on her door. There was a note to the milkman that she'd be back the next day. That's today, but she won't be back yet."

"What about the older Miss Gammer? You could have asked her."

Till supposed so.

"You could ask her now."

Till thought not. For one thing, it was too early in the morning.

"And for another thing," said Finder, "you're afraid."

Till said nothing.

"Why?"

Till mumbled.

"Speak up, boy."

Till said, "She might be a witch. She's so old that she's bent over like a witch, and she has a brindled cat, and she talks to herself, telling stories to her cat and to those hens of hers.

Her house is full of books, and some of the books look full of spells and witchcraft. She might really be a witch."

"Bosh, tosh, and rubbish!" said Finder. "That's no witch's cottage." Then, "I tell you what," he said as though he'd just had a brilliant idea that would delight Till. "I'll go halves with you on this job. One of us will get old Miss Gammer to come out of her house, and the other one will talk to her."

With his eyes Till measured the distance from where they stood to old Miss Gammer's back door. He would have to walk just so far under the witch-watching of those windows before knocking on that door. "I'd rather do the talking bit," said Till, "if you'll do the other."

"Agreed."

But Finder did not set off toward the house as Till expected. Instead, the old man stood just where he was and stretched out his left hand, flat, with the thumb tucked underneath, in the direction of old Miss Gammer's back door. And then several things happened all at the same time.

The whole of the house shivered and seemed to sway very slightly toward them.

A wild yowl rose from inside the house.

The cat flap in the back door flew up and stayed up.

Then a brindled cat rushed out through the opened cat door, yowling and spitting, every hair on end; it made straight for the nearest tree and was up the trunk and among the branches in a matter of seconds.

Till was still gaping at the cat, and Finder had just begun saying, "That's odd! I certainly didn't expect—" when old Miss Gammer's back door banged open. Through the doorway came old Miss Gammer herself in a red bathrobe and one slipper, just barely keeping her balance as she was blown forward, ending up face-to-face with Till.

She peered at him distractedly. "Till? It is Till, isn't it? An extra—a most extra—a most extraordinary thing! I was just going to make myself an early cup of tea; the kettle was in my hand, when—well, I can only describe it as an *indoor wind*—yes, an *indoor gale* blew me across the kitchen, out through the back door—to here! I've never known anything like it—never!" She was almost breathless with speech and excitement. "What an experience—what a tale to tell! But first you must let me—yes, you must let me collect myself!"

"Please do," said Till. The more flustered Miss Gammer was, the less witchlike she seemed. He needed only to keep his nerve and try to direct the rush of Miss Gammer's thoughts and words away from her recent startling experience toward the mystery of his lost dog, Bess. Did she know anything—anything at all—that could help?

He must find out what he needed to know without rudely badgering or bothering. He must be polite but politely persistent. He turned for help to Finder, who was standing beside him. But Finder was not standing beside him. He was nowhere to be seen in the whole of Gammers' Meadow.

Vanished.

Then Till remembered their agreement: his half of the job was to "do the talking," by himself.

And it turned out to be not so difficult, after all. Yes, old Miss Gammer remembered yesterday quite well. Nothing special, nothing like today's gale-force wind—quite amazing, that—but . . . a dog? Yes, she had heard a dog barking in the meadow yesterday. She hadn't seen it, but then she hadn't been looking out the window. . . . Here, for a moment, old Miss Gammer paused: she was thinking, she said, of the other Miss Gammer—yes, Mousy (as the elder Miss Gammer called her) might well have looked out the window, just before she left the house. You see, Mousy was always studying the view over the meadow. For her pictures, you know. So gifted. Always drawing . . . always painting . . .

Old Miss Gammer rambled on, unwitchlike, until she ran out of things to talk about. Then she said how nice it had been to hear all Till's news, which she did not often have a chance to do. But now she really must be getting home. She had some baking to do. Till must excuse her. And at last old Miss Gammer went back indoors.

Her cat did not follow her.

Till turned, and there was Finder at his side again. "You did well, boy," he said. "Yes, well done!"

"Miss Gammer said—" began Till.

"I heard it all," said Finder. "So now we know for certain that your little dog wasn't lost on her way to the meadow. As I supposed, she got here, since this Miss Gammer heard her barking. And the other Miss Gammer may even have seen her, too. You can ask her about that, if she's back later today."

"She is," said Till. "I told you."

"And you won't be afraid of *her*—the mousy Miss Gammer," said Finder.

"She's not mousy," said Till, "she's just Mousy. I mean," he went on hurriedly, for Finder had given an exasperated sigh, "old Miss Gammer calls her Mousy because

Mousy's her nickname. Mousy, because of the mice."

"The mice?"

"She does pictures for stories—all kinds of stories by other people. A lot of her pictures are of mice doing really clever, funny things. So she's Miss Mousy."

"Mice!" Finder shook his head. "The oddness—the weirdness—of human beings. Artists in particular, it seems."

Boldly, Till said, "Some people might think that Finders are, well, Strange People."

"Strange!" Finder was amused. "But we are *useful*." He dismissed the subject. "Meanwhile, to help us in our present search, I shall need to know much more about your Bess. You must tell me about her habits, her likes and dislikes, her favorite foods, and so on. Anything might come in handy."

So they sat down together in Gammers' Meadow among the buttercups and daisies, and Till told Finder about his dear dog, Bess. This time he shed no tears. He had hope.

Chapter 3
MUDMAN

As they sat in the meadow, Till told about Bess, and Finder listened carefully. At the same time, Finder was looking around him at what else was going on. He watched old Miss Gammer's hens, led hither and thither by their cockerel to peck in the grass. He noticed several ducks resting together on the riverbank. Wood pigeons swooped up and glided down from the trees. A heron flew over on some fishing expedition.

After Till had finished talking, Finder said, "Thank you." Then he got up without a further word and began to stroll about in the meadow. He did not seem to want company, so Till did not follow him.

Till had time to think as he watched him. He remembered his own words—"Strange People"—that he had said to Finder. He shivered a little, but not from fear. He was like his dog, Bess, who shivered all over when she thought that some new and daring adventure was about to begin.

Meanwhile, Finder had reached the riverbank and was walking along it, winding his way among the molehills,

his hands clasped behind his back. He
was apparently in deepest thought.

When Finder had completed his circuit
of the meadow, he came back to where Till was sitting.

"Many fish in the river?" he asked.

"Lots of minnows," said Till. "And I've seen bigger fish.
Miss Mousy says there are trout."

"But so difficult to get into any kind of real
communication"—Finder was talking to himself, and then
to Till—"with fish, I mean. No, we'd do better to try with
the birds in the meadow. And I
saw a squirrel just now:
another possibility. And
I noticed molehills, but—
well, moles keep to themselves.
Again, difficult."

"So will you—are you going to
ask the birds or the squirrels about Bess?"
Till was wide-eyed at the thought.

Finder shook his head. "If only it were as

simple as that. No, what we must have first is some kind of go-between—a suitable middleman, or rather, middle-thing. Some handy object that has been close to your little dog—if possible, loved by your little dog. You mentioned just now her special liking for some kind of plastic doll, I think it was?"

"Not a doll," said Till, "but she likes to take it to bed with her. She found it in the mud where the bank slopes down to the river."

"So it's from the mud of the river. It belongs here. Excellent."

"It's just some old toy," said Till. "I don't think it could ever have been a Batman or a Spider-Man, but perhaps something a little like that once. Now it's just rubbish—mud-rubbish."

"A Mudman, in fact. Where is it now?"

"In her dog basket. Shall I go home and fetch it? I could run."

"By no means," said Finder, alarmed. "This place and this day are all the time and space we have for our seeking. We must work within it. No, I'll bring Mudman to us—if I can."

He turned to face the direction from which they had come into Gammers' Meadow, and held out his left hand, palm upward, open. Nothing happened at once. Nothing, and after a while, from standing, Finder lowered himself to sitting on the grass, still holding his left hand out in the same position. He said, "I'm not as young as I was."

Till asked in a whisper, "You're very old, aren't you?"

"Just as old as my tongue and a little older than my teeth."

"What?"

"If you don't get it, you don't get it," said Finder.

"But what—?" said Till, still in a whisper.

"Hush!" said Finder loudly, sternly.

So Till stood in absolute silence, his eyes fixed on the open palm, delaying each blink of an eyelid in case he should miss anything—no, certainly something—that was going to happen.

The first thing that happened was a satisfied sigh from

Finder. The old man slowly, crankily, got to his feet, still holding his left hand in the same position, waiting.

Till stared on.

Then Till began to think that his sight must be fogging up from his staring. For there was a blurring of the palm of Finder's hand—or rather, a blur right *in* the palm.

The blur began to take shape . . . Shape . . . solidity. . . .

"Mudman!" Till breathed the name.

Yes, Mudman now lay there, at Finder's bidding, across the palm of Finder's left hand. He was only just recognizable as a toy. Limbs were missing; the head nodded a little in its socket; there were dog-tooth marks.

Finder poked at Mudman with the fingers of his right hand. "I think he'll do," he said. He held Mudman in his left hand for what seemed a long minute, then handed him to Till, who took him gingerly. And indeed Till felt a sharpish tingle as he touched Mudman, rather like the sting that had been in the garden gate when Finder had told him to open it. In an instant, however, that feeling passed.

"Let's try the hens first," said Finder. "Not too far off.

You can easily throw it to land among them, but—oh! Wait! Wait!"

But Till had not waited. With force he had thrown Mudman among the hens. He hit one of them—only her tail feathers, but the little flock scattered, squawking, the cockerel with them.

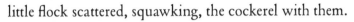

Finder waited for the birds' bitter outcry to lessen. Then, "I was going to say, boy, that you must remember you are only sending Mudman with a message, a civil question; you are not hurling a deadly missile."

"Oh," said Till. He fetched Mudman back.

"Try again, with the ducks this time," said Finder. "Remember to throw gently. Use an underhand lob. Lob gently."

"Right."

This time Till threw just as Finder directed, and Mudman landed neatly in a space in the middle of a little bevy of ducks by the river.

They were not at all flustered by his arrival, nor were they much interested. They looked at him for a moment, then, all together and without hurry, upped and waddled off and into the water.

"For some reason," said Finder, "they're simply not willing to take in the message I implanted. I wonder . . ." He was looking across the meadow to a willow tree on the riverbank. Under its shade a heron stood motionless, almost invisible. "Try him," said Finder.

Till was doubtful. "I'm not sure I could throw so far. At least, I don't think I could throw so far and accurately enough."

"Try, and you may discover that you can," said Finder. He laid his left hand on Till's shoulder in encouragement.

Till lobbed again. Mudman soared in the direction of the heron and landed at its feet.

The heron never moved.

Till held his breath.

Finder said, "Give him time. Herons are clever birds, but we all need time to think." Finder was watching the heron. "He will be taking in Mudman's message, the question I put. Then he will think about his answer—if he's willing to answer at all, that is. The ducks weren't willing—remember?"

At that moment the heron moved. It curved its long neck downward to pick Mudman up in its bill. Carrying the toy thus, like a fish to be eaten, the heron rose from the ground with flapping wings and started to fly toward where Till and Finder stood.

Finder suddenly said, "He's coming for you, boy—lie flat—quick!"

Till flung himself to the ground and, lying there, facedown, heard the scrape and sigh of wing feathers close overhead. Then there was a quite painful *thump!*—he found the bruise later—in the middle of his back. And the *whoosh!* of flight passed over him and on.

Slowly Till rolled over and sat up. He groped about for

Mudman, then realized that Finder was already holding him. He was holding him lightly and carefully in both hands. His eyes were shut, his face intent, as though he were listening to some indistinct sequence of sounds quite inaudible to Till.

Till waited.

Chapter 4
HOW HIGH SHE COULD JUMP

TILL WAITED WHILE FINDER HELD MUDMAN IN his hands, attending to whatever message was there for him. At first Finder was frowning at what he heard; then he began to snuffle to himself. Possibly he was laughing.

"What is it?" asked Till.

"Your little dog was always chasing around in the meadow, it seems, and barking, too—oh! Barking and barking and barking . . ."

Till was offended. "Lots of dogs do that," he said. "She chases the ducks, and she'd chase the hens if I'd let her. But she's never caught up with any of them. She only frightens them."

"Frightens them? No!" said Finder. "According to the heron, she scares nobody but disturbs everybody. The ducks take to the water, other birds fly up into the air, and the squirrels stay in their treetops. And the heron itself—I won't repeat to you its opinion of your noisy little dog."

"It's not fair," said Till. "She isn't like that all the time. Sometimes she plays with me, and then she's clever and quick and quiet. When we're both tired out, I sit down and she lies down against me, quite still and quiet, resting. And sometimes she creeps into my lap—she's just the right size—and curls around there, and then, when I lay my hand on her to stroke her, I can feel her heart beating."

Till put his hands up to his face to stop his tears from coming.

Finder said gently, "Tell me more about her. Describe her."

So Till described Bess: the smallness of her and the color she was; the feel of her coat when he stroked her, and the velvet feel of her ears; the set of her ears; the wag of her tail; her inquisitive nose and the way the soft, black, damp end of it twitched when she was taking in the different smells of the meadow. How fast she could run and how high she could jump.

"And the games you play together?" asked Finder.

So Till told Finder about ball games with Bess and then about hiding from Bess behind a tree trunk and always

being found. And then, when Till
swung on the tire to and fro—*up
and down, up and down*—Bess would run alongside it,
jumping to and fro—*up and down, up and down*—
trying to catch a loose end of the rope as it flew
past with the swinging.

"I can imagine," said Finder. "Something like
that, wasn't it?" And he turned toward the tree with the tire
swing hanging from it. He was pointing at it with the
forefinger of his left hand.

Till turned to look in the same direction.

He saw Bess—he really *saw* his own dear Bess—racing
to and fro with the swinging of the tire. "Oh!" he shouted
for joy, but instantly saw who was also there, swinging on
the tire—a boy, himself, Till.

"No," he whispered, bewildered, fearful. Then, even as
he looked, boy and dog were no longer there. The tire hung
motionless on its rope. No one, nothing, was near it.

"What was it?" he whispered. "I saw—I really *saw*—Bess, and me, a ghost. I shall be dead and be a ghost. . . ."

"Nonsense," said Finder. "You really saw, but what you saw was not really there. I was allowing you to see what I was seeing in my mind's eye—in my imagination. And I could see it in my imagination only because you had described it to me so well. I could see it, and then you saw what I saw. That's all there is to it."

"That's all," repeated Till, reassured, but only for a moment. Then: "That's all? There was no Bess—there is no Bess, still! Really and truly, I have lost her. . . ."

"No," said Finder. "It's true that the birds of the meadow have failed us. That only means that we must work harder to unearth the truth." Till saw that Finder was amused at something. He was snuffling again.

"What is it?" asked Till.

"If you don't get it, you may yet," said Finder. With Mudman still in his hand, he had begun to move away from the swing toward the riverbank.

Till followed him. 🐍

Chapter 5
STRANGE FOOTSTEPS

When they came to the molehills on the riverbank, Finder slowed his pace. From molehill to molehill he went, like a hound questing. He stopped by one that seemed to Till exactly like all the others, but this was the one Finder had decided upon. He lowered himself to the ground and—having laid Mudman aside—began to remove the earth, handful by handful, very carefully, beginning from the top of the molehill. To Till he said, "Set to, boy! You can help."

Wondering, Till joined in the work.

As they worked to dismantle the molehill, Finder explained to Till that, at the base and center of every such hill, there is a hole up through which a mole has pushed the waste earth from its underground tunnelings.

"And here, I think—yes!—here's the hole!" said Finder.

When the hole was quite cleared of surrounding earth, Finder picked up Mudman, holding the figure to him with a lingering care. It looked more battered than ever from being thrown to and fro so much recently. The head had loosened even further.

"Now, my Mudman!"
Finder was trying
Mudman for size:
probably he could be
pushed down the hole and
into the tunnel—just barely.
But he could not be pushed very
far: Finder's ancient, knobbly hand
was too stiff and awkward for the job.

"You try, boy."

Till's hand was smaller and could make itself smaller still. He pushed Mudman, headfirst, right into the hole and down.

"Go on!" Finder urged. "Push as far as you possibly can, but never lose the grip on your end. Hold on tight. Tight."

So Till pushed on until his forearm was swallowed up almost to the elbow and he was panting with the effort.

"Now we must wait," Finder said. "Every mole lives alone in its own tunnels. Every mole hates—positively *hates*—visitors. So when this mole realizes its private

burrow has been invaded by a stranger, smelling of dog and boy and heron and I don't know what else—"

Till interrupted. "Something's happening. I can feel Mudman being pushed back from the other end!"

"Hold him fast where he is!" Finder was excited. "The mole has to receive my message—the whole of it. There's my question, and I have added to it a condition: Mudman does not leave this tunnel without an answer for us. So hold fast, boy!"

They were both crouching so closely over the molehill that they could now hear the angry twittering, sometimes rising almost to a squeal, of the infuriated mole below.

Then suddenly all went quiet: the resistance to Till's pushing ceased; he dared to relax his hold a little.

A long pause.

Then, without warning, Mudman shot out backward from the hole, covering Till with fine dirt and causing him to give a shout of alarm.

But Finder was delighted: "I think our mole has seen

sense. If so . . . " He had reached to pick up Mudman, now in a pitiable state indeed: earth-stained, with mole-teeth marks added to the dog's, and the distraught head lolling on the shoulders. Finder nursed this object in his hands attentively, bending his head close, as if listening.

At last, hesitantly, he began: "The mole remembers— yes, quite certainly the mole speaks of yesterday and what it became aware of then. Footfalls."

Till said very quickly, "Bess's?"

"No. And that's not surprising. A dog would be too light-footed to make the earth tremble: nothing would be felt below."

"Oh." Till desponded.

"The mole heard *you,* however—a boy's footsteps that it recognized from many times before. This time they were running to and fro in what the mole thought was some unusual—some, perhaps, frantic—way."

"I'd lost her," said Till. "Oh, I knew I'd lost her!"

Finder said, "But even before your running footsteps— and this is of the greatest importance—the mole heard other footsteps on the riverbank that were quite unfamiliar to it. The footsteps of a strange person—that's exactly how the mole puts it. The footsteps of a strange person."

Till saw that there was more to come.

Finder said, "So far, so good. But then immediately the mole also speaks of the same strange footsteps today. That makes no sense. The dew was still everywhere in the meadow, undisturbed, when we entered it. Nobody else has been here today on the riverbank. Only ourselves."

Till wondered something but said nothing.

Finder said, "The only explanation is that the mole confuses today with yesterday. The creature lives always alone and always in the dark. No wonder it becomes muddleheaded about time."

"But . . ." began Till. He simply could not believe that this mole was muddleheaded. He remembered his hand gripping Mudman in that deep mole-darkness underground—his hand separated only by the length of Mudman's body from the jaws and claws of the resolute mole. The mole then had seemed a very clearheaded animal

indeed as it worked to dislodge Mudman from its tunnel entrance.

Finder saw that Till was troubled. "Well, boy?"

There were questions that Till wanted to ask, but Finder was unimaginably old and magical—and touchy.

"Well, boy? Out with it."

Till picked on words that had bothered him. "The mole said that, on both days, there were footsteps of a Strange Person."

"Yes, a stranger on the riverbank."

"A Strange Person on the riverbank."

"That's what I said."

"Oh."

"What does that 'oh' mean?"

"Nothing—nothing." Till did not dare to argue.

Finder said, "We have time here, but not much. Waste none of it in quibbling over words, boy." Till remained silent, so Finder continued, "Mudman has gained us some useful information: there was indeed an intruder in the meadow yesterday. *What was that intruder up to?*"

Finder was baffled by his own question.

Till watched as the old man turned slowly around to view each part of the meadow in turn, as if the answer to his question must lie there. He ended up facing the Gammer cottages. He said, more to himself than to Till, "I could try again for an eyewitness. This time for a creature of superior intelligence, and—if possible—unprejudiced."

He mused.

Then, "Tell me, boy—your noisy little dog"—Till opened his mouth but shut it again before there was time for his protest to come out—"your Bess, did she ever bark at old Miss Gammer's cat?"

"Never."

"Never chased it?"

"Her cat was always indoors, sitting in the window, looking out."

"A watcher, as cats are. A natural witness. And likely to be neutral." Finder nodded to himself. "Come!" Still clasping Mudman to him, the old man set off across the meadow again in the direction of the cottages.

Chapter 6
THE BRINDLED CAT

 TILL HAD FORGOTTEN

about old Miss Gammer's cat, which had been blown out of her house ahead of her and taken refuge in the nearest tall tree. But Finder had not forgotten: the cat's behavior at the time had puzzled him.

Now, with Mudman in his hand, he went to stand under the tree and look upward into its leafy top. In a low voice he called to Till to join him. "Your eyes are better than mine. Is the brindled cat still there?"

Till tipped his head back to search the tree-world above him with his eyes. He could see nothing but boughs and branches and twigs and leaves. Then something different.

He whispered to Finder, "I think I can see it—just about."

"And what's it doing?"

"Watching us."

"As it was, depend upon it, when we were among the molehills. And earlier, too, of course."

He shook his head slowly. "An eyewitness, certainly, but I have my doubts. But then again, perhaps . . ."

Finder moved away from the tree until he was out of earshot of any listener there. Till had followed him. "Doubts?"

"Misgivings. The old lady is no witch, but her cat—you saw how it behaved earlier. Tell me, did old Miss Gammer have it as a kitten?"

"No. It was already half grown—a stray. How it came to her is one of her stories."

"Tell me."

"I can't do it as she does it."

"Never mind. Tell."

"She always says it was a most terrible night: storm—rain, hail, thunder, lightning—everything. Oh, and a high wind was blowing things down and about, and there's a great *slam!* as something's blown hard against her back door. Then there was a lull in the storm, and Miss Gammer

hears this tiny noise like a human child crying, but tiny—
tiny—tiny . . ."

"Go on."

"So she opens her door a crack, and outside on the
doorstep is the wretchedest thing you could think of. Just a
heap of wet hair or feathers or fur—she didn't know which
until she picked it up, and there were bones under fur, and
teeth—and the teeth bit her. But she held on and brought
the creature indoors into the light and the warmth, and lo
and behold! It wasn't some hairy little demon at all, but a
young cat. A young cat with only one eye."

"So?"

"Old Miss Gammer says she thought at once that it
might be a witch's cat turned out by its mistress for
something wrong it had done."

"Only one eye," said Finder thoughtfully. "The other lost
in a parting blow from a broomstick?"

"Perhaps," said Till. "Anyway, that's Miss Gammer's
story of the cat. And the cat's chosen to live with Miss
Gammer ever since, just as if it were an ordinary cat."

"No ordinary cat, I fancy. And here lies our difficulty: an ordinary cat—as you call it—can be playful, sly, even mischievous. But a witch cat! There one meets a trained intelligence, a subtler, crueler, *wickeder* sense of humor. A delight in deception and disappointment. Expect no favors from a witch cat."

"So you won't ask it anything?"

"I won't directly—I can't, anyway, as I explained to you at the start. But we still have our go-between, our faithful Mudman. With Mudman I can perhaps tempt even this cat into telling us something useful."

Till watched as Finder turned his attention to Mudman again. First of all he held Mudman against himself, closely, almost lovingly. Then, with his back to the tree, he began to work at Mudman's wagging head to loosen it still further. He wriggled it and wrenched at it.

"Ouch!" said Till under his breath as at last the head came free of the body. Completely detached from the rest of Mudman, it appeared roughly round, roughly ball-shaped. Finder carried these two objects—the head-ball and the body—as he resumed his seemingly idle walking. This brought him to within a short distance from the foot of the tree on the side nearest to Miss Gammer's back door. There he let both parts of Mudman fall, as though he were tired of carrying a broken toy.

Finder whispered to Till, "There are some things that a cat—even a witch cat—can't resist. Come away now, and we'll watch from a distance."

He strolled on with Till, as if they had lost interest in the tree and the cat. They paused some way off, apparently to admire the view, but they could still look sideways at the tree and, beneath it, at Mudman and his severed head.

After a while Till began to say, "I don't think—"

"Quiet!" said Finder. "Look!"

The brindled cat was coming down the trunk of the tree very carefully, backward. It sprang the last few feet to the ground and then sat there, grooming itself.

They waited.

After a time the cat got up

and began to make its way toward old Miss Gammer's back door. It came to Mudman, thrown away on the ground, with his head lying a little apart from his body. The cat seemed hardly to glance at the ruined thing but sauntered past, its thoughts elsewhere. Then its pace became even more leisurely; it slowed, stopped.

The cat turned back, as if an idea had just occurred to it. It was now approaching Mudman and his ball-shaped head. Very close now, the cat paused again and gazed. Then it stretched out a long paw to tap at the head-ball. The head-ball did not move. Then the cat curled its paw around the head-ball and pulled it sideways a little. The head-ball rolled very slightly, and at once the cat pounced upon it.

Now the cat began to play in earnest with its ball. It patted it, struck it away, pursued it, and captured it; rolled it and trundled it; biffed it and batted it; and even threw it into the air. It seemed as if the cat gave the head-ball a life of its own, and now Till began to notice that, left to itself on the ground for an instant, the head-ball always rolled slowly or fast in one favored direction. Perhaps the ground sloped. Whatever the reason, the head-ball always rolled back from wherever it was toward the body and came to rest there.

So the cat always had to go back to the body to retrieve its toy. Its sport continued, until surely the creature must have been tiring. It was reaching out, for what turned out to be the last time, to get the head-ball back when it happened to place its reaching paw not on the head-ball but on the body.

The effect was instantaneous and remarkable.

The cat became absolutely still, like a statue of a cat. After a while, slowly, the cat reached out a second fore-paw to rest on the body, and there the two paws stayed, side by side. And there the cat stayed, crouched over the body of Mudman, unmoving, for what seemed to Till a long, long time.

Abruptly the cat stood up, away from Mudman's body, and yawned. Without a further glance at Mudman, body or head, it walked slowly, daintily, toward old Miss Gammer's back door. It raised the cat flap and slithered through.

Finder and Till hurried to Mudman. Till picked up the head; Finder picked up the body and, as usual, listened.

"Well?"

Finder listened on. Then slowly he began to repeat the message aloud: *"Pussycat, pussycat, where have you been?"*

He paused.

Till said, "But that's just an old nursery rhyme—the beginning of it."

"Not 'just an old nursery rhyme,'" Finder said gloomily. "Oh, this turns out to be a nursery rhyme with a difference! Trust a witch cat to twist a simple rhyme into a riddle—a puzzle that—"

He was interrupted. One of old Miss Gammer's windows was flung open, and she leaned out to call, "Mousy's back from town! Mousy's back, and there's to be a cream tea—a feast!"

"Aha!" said Finder. And from the tone of his voice, Till knew that he had at once given up worrying about the brindled cat's nursery rhyme. Nor did cream teas interest him. No, Finder was relying on what Miss Mousy might be able to tell about a dog barking in the meadow just before she left for town. ✍

Chapter 7
MISS MOUSY

TILL WAS WORRIED—WORRIED THAT NEITHER OF the Miss Gammers had met Finder so far. Miss Mousy had not the slightest idea of his existence. Old Miss Gammer, on the other hand, might have seen him when they were criss-crossing the meadow earlier, or she might possibly have noticed him just now, when she opened the window to call the news of Miss Mousy's return. But Till rather thought not.

What were the two Miss Gammers going to make of such a—well, such an *unusual*-looking friend for Till?

But Finder, with Till hanging back only a very little, was already following old Miss Gammer: she had popped out of her back door and then in through the back door of Miss Mousy's cottage. Here she was now, ahead of them, in Miss Mousy's kitchen, helping Miss Mousy with her shopping, which still hung about her in parcels and bags. In town, Miss Mousy had been stocking up on drawing paper and pencils and pens and colors—anything that an artist might need in her work. A few little extras, too—little luxuries.

Till was relieved that, during the bustle in Miss

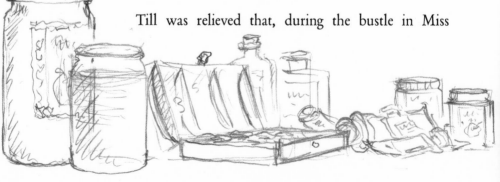

Mousy's kitchen, Finder chose to remain in the background, unnoticed. He did, however, whisper to Till, "You know what you have to ask her. Now is the time. Ask."

So Till did.

"Oh, yes," said Miss Mousy, "certainly I heard your little dog in the meadow. I'd know that bark anywhere, although—" She broke off to warn old Miss Gammer. "Careful with that package, dear. It's the Cornish cream."

"But, Miss Mousy, did you *see* my Bess?"

"As soon as—well, almost as soon as I heard the barking, I glanced out into the meadow, because—" Again she interrupted herself with an afterthought for old Miss Gammer: "You've still got a pot of the raspberry jam to go with the cream, I hope?"

Old Miss Gammer said she had, and would fetch it in due course.

Till had lost his grip on the conversation. Now Finder spoke for him: "So you saw the little dog in the meadow, ma'am?"

His question drew the attention of the two Miss Gammers to their extra visitor. For the first time they looked at Finder

properly. They stared at him as he stood there, holding the headless body of Mudman.

Miss Mousy said, "Till, you have not introduced us."

Before Till could speak—and he hardly knew what to say, anyway—Finder had stepped forward with something like a bow. "A Finder at your service, ma'am." In a vaguely gallant gesture, he flourished his left hand in the air, attempting at the same time a fluttering of the fingers. The forefinger—the finger with the ring on it—ended up pointing straight at Miss Mousy. She gave a little "Oh!" of surprise and sat down suddenly on one of her kitchen chairs.

Finder spoke: "You say you heard the little dog barking in the meadow, ma'am. Then you looked out into the meadow?"

Choosing her words carefully, Miss Mousy said, "Yes, Mr. Affeinder, I did. Now, why exactly did I do that? Oh, yes. Partly because Till's little dog was barking, perhaps rather oddly. And even odder was, when I looked, I couldn't see her there—I mean, on the riverbank, where the barking seemed to be coming from. But I'm afraid I forgot her when—when I saw . . ."

Finder prompted her: "Yes?"

"You know, I've so often painted that landscape—but yesterday morning it interested me in a new, strange way. So strange that—though I was in a hurry for town—I stopped then and there to make a quick pencil sketch. Just as a reminder. Now, where's that sketch pad?" Miss Mousy began to scrabble among the objects on her kitchen table.

While she scrabbled, Till saw—out of the corner of his eye—that old Miss Gammer slipped out of the kitchen to go back into her own cottage.

Miss Mousy found her sketch pad and flipped it open. "There!"

The three of them gazed down at the landscape on the page.

Miss Mousy had dashed off her sketch in pencil, with written notes to herself on the colors to be used later. The meadow itself was marked with the word "sunlit." The trees massed on the farther riverbank were to be "v. dark grn?" And between the trees and the meadow foreground, seemingly from the riverbank itself, a strong upward stroke sprang, appearing as "pale yellow?" against the dark of the trees.

skyblue

sap
grn

SUNLIT

Light
Red

"An absolute vertical of lighter color against the dark," said Miss Mousy. "Quite dramatic. I can't quite work out what it actually was, to produce such an effect. So straight, so upright, so slender—no, it's a mystery. And then something much more mysterious."

Till only breathed the name: "Bess?"

"No," said Miss Mousy. "Something else . . ."

"Yes?" said Finder, since Miss Mousy had hesitated.

"I was, of course, sketching against time, anyway. I was looking up at the view, then quickly down to my pad—up and down—and suddenly I looked up, and this rather lovely vertical effect was no longer there. Gone. Totally vanished."

"But you're certain it was there to begin with?"

"Oh, yes!"

"Not just a trick of the sunlight?"

"No."

"Not something you might have imagined?"

"Certainly not."

Till asked, "And what about my Bess?"

"Still nowhere to be seen. And the barking had become irregular, muffled."

At this point old Miss Gammer rejoined the party, bringing with her from her kitchen a whiff of something hot, dry, and delicious.

Miss Mousy raised inquiring eyebrows. "Scones?"

"Doing nicely," said old Miss Gammer.

"For tea," Miss Mousy explained to the others. "Although," she added, puzzled, "I don't seem to remember having had lunch earlier."

Or breakfast, thought Till. But he knew that this was no ordinary day with ordinary mealtimes. This was Finder's day.

"Anyway," said Miss Mousy, "surely a cream tea is always welcome. And I hope that you will join us, Mr. Affeinder, as well as Till here."

"Delighted," said Finder. But Till could see that he was disappointed in what Miss Mousy had told them. It was so little, and it only deepened the mystery of Bess's disappearance.

Finder sighed, then seemed to come to a decision. He turned to old Miss Gammer. "You are the scholar, ma'am, I believe? Deep in book learning, no doubt?"

"You flatter me, Mr. Affeinder."

Finder disregarded her protest. "No doubt you know the rhyme that begins, *Pussycat, pussycat, where have you been?*"

"Of course. That hardly needs book learning, as you call it." She finished the rhyme for him:

"I've been to London to visit the Queen.

Pussycat, pussycat, what did you there?

I frightened a little mouse under her chair."

"Thank you, ma'am," said Finder. "But are you aware of your own cat's version of that same rhyme?"

"My cat! My Brindy? What do you mean?"

This time Finder addressed them all. "Let me explain," he said. ✦

Chapter 8
PUZZLERS

TO EXPLAIN TO THE MISS GAMMERS, FINDER went back to the beginning of the story of the search for Bess. He told them about the choice of Mudman as go-between and showed them his battered, headless body. Then he told them about the hens, the ducks, and the heron; and then about the molehill and the mole; and finally came to the brindled cat and the head-ball.

At this point in Finder's story, Till held out Mudman's severed head. Finder took it and showed how it had once fitted onto Mudman's body. Then he laid aside the two parts on Miss Mousy's kitchen table, giving a little farewell *tap!* to the head with the forefinger of his left hand.

In Finder's telling of his story to the Miss Gammers, Till had noticed how much he left out — particularly such parts as could have bewildered or even alarmed them. Then Finder reached the nursery rhyme itself, and almost at once old Miss Gammer interrupted him: "You say that Brindy repeated the rhyme with a difference? So Brindy spoke, and you understood?"

"Yes."

The brindled cat had slid into the kitchen without anyone's noticing and was now twisting itself around old Miss Gammer's ankles. Miss Gammer addressed it directly: "Brindy—my Brindy! How could you favor a stranger so, and speak to him, and never to me? Oh, Brindy!" In loving reproach she stooped to stroke her cat, but the cat had at once moved off to a distance and there sat down with its back to them all. The tip of its tail twitched.

"You forget, ma'am," said Finder. "Your cat could speak only through Mudman, to me alone, and not in words that ears could hear. The boy standing by me heard nothing."

"Only what you told me," said Till.

Old Miss Gammer said, "Will you tell us what you call Brindy's version of the nursery rhyme?"

"Certainly," said Finder, "and make of it what you can." He cleared his throat and began:

"Pussycat, pussycat, where have you been?
I at the window watching two that were green.
Pussycat, pussycat, what made you stare?
A little dog barking who wasn't there."

A silence fell in Miss Mousy's kitchen—a silence, except that the brindled cat had begun a pleased purring.

Finder said, "I had hoped that, between the four of us, we might . . ." His voice faded into its own forlorn silence. The only sound left was the purring of the cat.

"You are quite right, Mr. Affeinder," said Miss Mousy, suddenly determined. "Four intelligent people should not be beaten by a mere nonsense rhyme."

Finder shook his head. "Not mere nonsense, ma'am. A puzzle set deliberately to mislead us."

"Puzzle!" exclaimed old Miss Gammer. "Do you remember, Mousy, all those crossword puzzles we solved together? It was often simpler than one expected," she explained to the others. "Just a matter of looking closely at the words of a clue to see what meanings might be there.

For instance, the second line of this rhyme: *I at the window watching two that were green.* Now, what greenness could a cat see from my kitchen window?"

"Only the whole meadow," said Finder gloomily.

Old Miss Gammer dared to ignore him. She said, "Green animals? I think not. Not in our meadow."

"Nor green people," said Miss Mousy.

"Unless," said Till under his breath, "magical people." He glanced at Finder, but Finder did not meet his gaze.

Miss Mousy tried to cheer them all: "Working on a particular crossword clue, we might be stumped. Then we'd leave that clue to try another that looked easier. They all connected up in the end."

"So," said old Miss Gammer, "we might leave *two that were green* and look at the earlier part of the same line: *I at the window watching . . .*

Very straightforward that, I think. No hidden meanings there." She sighed.

Till remarked, "I'd have said, *Me at the window watching . . .*"

"Less correct," said old Miss Gammer. "Never having heard Brindy speak, I don't know how fussy he would be about grammar."

"*I at the window . . .*" Miss Mousy repeated slowly. "It does sound rather—well, stiff. I wonder . . . We have only *heard* that line through Mr. Affeinder—we've never seen it written down. Nor did he see it written down, I think. Mr. Affeinder?"

"No," said Finder. "No, I didn't."

"So that first word might not be *I* meaning 'myself'; it could actually be *eye*—spelled *e-y-e.*"

"Brindy's eye—his one eye!" cried old Miss Gammer. "*Eye at the window watching*—yes!"

"If so," said Miss Mousy, "the one eye at the beginning of the line perhaps means that the two at the end are also eyes: *two* eyes *that were green.*"

"And very few people have really green eyes," said old

Miss Gammer. "It should be easy to track down such a person. And then, of course—"

"Not so fast!" said Finder. "How close do you have to be to see the color of a person's eyes?"

"Oh . . ." said old Miss Gammer thoughtfully.

"Ah . . ." said Miss Mousy, equally thoughtful.

Till said nothing, but the Miss Gammers saw the disappointment in his face. Old Miss Gammer said, "If we were quite baffled, we'd leave the crossword altogether, for the time being."

"Come back to it later," Miss Mousy said cheerfully, "with fresh ideas."

And at that the two Miss Gammers parted, old Miss Gammer to go next door to check the scones in her oven, and Miss Mousy to remain to tidy away the rest of her shopping. Old Miss Gammer came back and joined in the tidying. Finder and Till could not help them, so they watched them. The brindled cat also watched.

Miss Mousy came across her sketchbook and was reminded that old Miss Gammer had never seen the landscape with the mysterious vertical. She showed it to her now. Old Miss Gammer peered, then said, "Surely it's just some kind of pole."

"So I thought at first. But why on earth should there suddenly be a pole just there on the riverbank? No, it makes no sense."

Old Miss Gammer, however, had been swept back into crossword mode: "What kinds of poles are there, anyway? Maypoles? Telegraph poles?"

"Too big—far too big for the thing I saw. Look again."

A quick glance at the sketch, then old Miss Gammer rattled on: "Tent pole? Vaulting pole? Punt pole? Beanpole?"

"Stop! That's it—that's it!"

"What? Runner beans climbing up poles on our riverbank?"

"No—of course not! The pole before that."

"Punt pole?"

"That's it!"

Till had been listening closely, hopefully. He said, "But where's the punt, then?"

"One wouldn't see it," said Miss Mousy. "On the river, of course, but below eye level. Made fast against the riverbank by the punt pole driven into the river bottom. Moored there for a landing. Oh, it certainly makes sense now—I mean, what I saw."

"So someone came punting up the river," said Old Miss Gammer.

"And saw Till's little dog in our meadow and fancied her," said Miss Mousy.

"And absolutely had to have her," said old Miss Gammer. "And now I see where the green eyes fit in: Green-Eyed Jealousy. Whoever-It-Was had eyes that turned green with envy, as the saying goes, when they saw Till's dog."

"Eye at the window watching two that were green," quoted Miss Mousy. "We've solved that riddle! And look! The cat's in a huff that we've done it."

The brindled cat was stalking out of Miss Mousy's

kitchen and into her back garden. Unmistakably it was displeased.

A moment of triumph for the Gammers, and then it ended.

Miss Mousy was still staring at the sketch in her sketch-book.

Old Miss Gammer said, "Mousy?"

"That punt pole still bothers me," said Miss Mousy.

Till said, "But it had to be there. For the punt. You explained."

"Oh, it was there all right—I saw it. The trouble is— one moment it was there; the next, not. It vanished. But I never saw anyone taking it. How could that be?"

Nobody answered her question, but Till said, "Somehow, somebody took the punt pole, and that person is Whoever-It-Was who stole my Bess."

Chapter 9
WHOEVER-IT-WAS

⟡ IN THE TALK OF GREEN-EYED JEALOUSY AND A
punt pole, Finder had taken no part. He had been darkly
silent—perhaps thinking ahead of the other three. But now
he listened with attention to what Till had to say.

"Suppose—just suppose someone could disappear
whenever they wanted. . . ."

Till was thinking back to when he and Finder had stood
together outside old Miss Gammer's cottage, waiting for her
to come out and be questioned. Till had agreed to do the
questioning, so it was fair enough for Finder to absent
himself, if he wanted. But how? One moment Finder was
there; the next, not. And when old Miss Gammer had gone
back indoors, instantly there he was again. Moreover, it
seemed that Finder had overheard all the conversation
between Till and Miss Gammer. There was only one
possible explanation: Finder had not gone away at all; he
had simply made himself invisible.

Was Whoever-It-Was another Strange Person,
like Finder himself, with the same
powers of invisibility?

Aloud, Till said, "If Miss Gammer's cat is telling the truth—"

"Well!" said old Miss Gammer, but Miss Mousy shushed her.

"If the cat is telling the truth," said Till, "it saw Whoever-It-Was come punting along the river and finding my Bess in the meadow. And the cat saw Whoever-It-Was green with envy for her and planning to steal her. All just as you've said. But Whoever-It-Was must be quick, because Bess's owner might turn up at any moment. So, for safety, Whoever-It-Was decides on invisibility."

Till paused, for at the word *invisibility* the two Miss Gammers had flinched, but they had already believed too many impossible things that day to be daunted by this one. "And, of course," Till went on, "a little dog who's picked up and held by someone invisible becomes invisible, too."

"But not inaudible," Miss Mousy said eagerly. "I heard her barking. So, without even trying, we've solved the riddle at the end of the nursery rhyme:

"A little dog barking who wasn't there."

"And invisibility explains about the punt pole, too," said Till. "As long as Whoever-It-Was wasn't holding it, you could see it. Then Whoever-It-Was came back to the riverbank, invisible and carrying an invisible dog, and took hold of the pole to use it, and at once that pole vanished."

Old Miss Gammer finished the story: "Then into the punt with the punt pole and the kidnapped dog, and away! The villain!"

"And we still don't know who that villain is," said Miss Mousy.

Till said, "There's one clue left to help us: what the mole remembered." He looked anxiously at Finder, knowing that Finder refused to take seriously all that the mole had told them. Strange footfalls yesterday—yes; the same strange footfalls today—impossible. The mole had misremembered and muddled, according to Finder.

According to Finder.

Till stared at Finder, willing him to speak out—or at least to look at him. But Finder looked steadfastly away and said nothing.

A hideous thought that had lived at the back of Till's mind for some time was worming its way to the front. Here it was now. Till said to Finder, "Those footsteps—the footsteps the mole recognized—they were yours, weren't they, today *and yesterday*? There was only one Strange Person, and it was you. You came yesterday by punt and stole my Bess, and you came again today, pretending to help me find her. I don't know why you should do such a thing, but you did."

At last Finder turned his head.

He said, "Look me in the face, boy."

Till looked.

"Into my eyes."

Till looked.

Finder said, "I never played you such a cruel, silly trick."

Slowly Till answered, "No. You didn't. Of course you didn't." Then, "But you know Whoever-It-Was who came yesterday."

"Yes. I know—now. And I should have guessed earlier," said Finder. "Someone as close to me as another self from the very day we two were born, someone with my same footfalls, with my same powers; always my envious enemy—my brother—my twin brother. Like me he is a Finder, but one of the Finders Keepers, which I am not. And yesterday he found, and now very certainly he hopes to keep."

Finder was angry, but he did not shout or roar his anger. He spoke quietly, but—as old Miss Gammer said afterward—as if in larger and larger capital letters. He said, "I shall go to him. I shall HAVE IT OUT WITH HIM.

I shall TEACH HIM WHAT'S WHAT and

WHOSE IS WHOSE."

He was very angry, and anger seemed to make him swell. Finder was not a big man, but Miss Mousy thought that he now appeared to grow so tall that his head was about to knock against her kitchen ceiling. A towering rage indeed!

Miss Mousy feared for the safety of the breakables and other things in her little kitchen. Already Mudman had been whirled off her kitchen table by a gust of Finder's fury. So she set about edging her visitors out of her kitchen, through her back door, and into her back garden. From its refuge tree, the brindled cat watched their coming.

By now Finder had calmed himself to speak almost as usual: "Boy!"

Till was frightened, but he stepped forward.

"You shall have your dog again," said Finder. "Trust me. But to get her back, I need two things. First, some proof that I can show of your ownership of the dog. Second, something of value to you that you offer in exchange."

Till stared at Finder, bewildered.

Finder said more gently, "Begin with the second thing. You must think of something precious to give in exchange for your Bess."

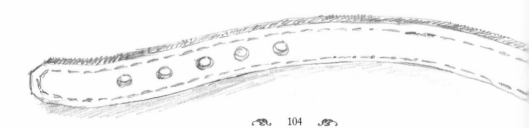

In dismay, Till cried, "But here—now—I have nothing. Nothing!"

At once the two Miss Gammers intervened with offers of something valuable from their own cottages—a silver spoon, a ruby ring—anything they possessed.

Sternly, Finder swept their offers aside. "The thing must be his."

Then Till remembered the new collar. He pulled it from his pocket. It was an expensive, handsome thing, made of strong, shiny, brown leather with a good brass ring for attachment to a leash; a band of brass went partway around it and twinkled in the sunshine.

He handed the collar over.

Finder turned it, reading something written along the brasswork. "Here's your name and address, boy."

"Yes," said Till.

"And the same will be somewhere on the old collar that your dog still wears?"

"Oh, yes," said Till.

"Then this is proof of ownership. I need nothing more."

Then Finder was bidding them good-bye. They hardly heard the words of his farewell for what happened afterward—but instantaneously afterward. It was, as old Miss Gammer said later, as though the air took a sudden gigantic gulp of itself, so that the Miss Gammers and Till were flung violently together, clutching one another to keep their footing. The brindled cat was among them, clawing and spitting.

Then the paroxysm of the air subsided; the cat had fled to its tree again; the others were left gasping and tottering. The three of them began to sort themselves out and to realize that the fourth was no longer with them.

Finder had gone. ✧

Chapter 10
BESS

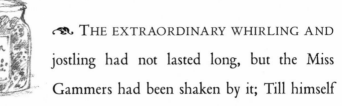

 THE EXTRAORDINARY WHIRLING AND jostling had not lasted long, but the Miss Gammers had been shaken by it; Till himself seemed low-spirited. Nobody wanted to discuss what had happened—or what might happen next.

Miss Mousy was the first to recover. She tried to rouse the others by starting preparations for her cream tea party. She said she would like her garden table and chairs to be set out for four, and meanwhile she would put the kettle on.

There was nothing else to do, so Till began arranging the chairs. He spread the tablecloth that Miss Mousy brought out to him and carried cups and saucers for her.

Old Miss Gammer had gone back into her cottage to fetch the scones and the raspberry jam to go on the tea table. Then she went into Miss Mousy's kitchen to help there. Almost at once she was out again, smiling broadly and holding something hidden behind her back.

"Till, guess what I found on the floor under Mousy's kitchen table?"

"What?"

She held it out to him: "Mudman!"

"Oh," Till said.

"But don't you see, Till? This is Mudman whole, with his head back on his body again, as if it had always been there. It's magic, Till—Mr. Affeinder's magic."

Then Till remembered that gnarled, ringed forefinger and the gentle *tap!* to the head-ball as it lay against Mudman's shoulders. All the same, he did not offer to take Mudman, so Miss Gammer set the toy more or less upright in the middle of the tea table. She said, "Mr. Affeinder mended him so that your Bess could have her doll when she's back with you again."

Till said nothing.

Old Miss Gammer said sharply, "Till, you're not still afraid you'll never have your Bess again?"

Till said, "When he said good-bye, he said, 'This is good-bye' in such a final sort of way. As though he were never coming back."

"But he'd also promised you your dog. He'd said, 'Trust me.' Don't you trust him, Till?"

Then Till cried out, "I'm in such a muddle—I don't know—I just don't know!"

At that moment Miss Mousy called to them to help her with the last of the tea things.

The cat came down from its tree and sat on the fourth chair. Miss Mousy explained that it was always allowed a teaspoonful of cream.

Miss Mousy had brewed the tea and now began pouring it out. "We needn't wait for a latecomer," she said.

Old Miss Gammer was urging Till to try one of her scones—still warm from the oven—with the clotted cream and jam. Till was saying he wasn't hungry.

Suddenly the brindled cat opened its mouth and mewed loudly.

Old Miss Gammer was startled. "Brindy never meows," she said.

"Something he heard or saw that he didn't like?" suggested Miss Mousy.

They all looked around and listened: nothing was unusual.

Miss Mousy scooped the teaspoonful of cream and laid it on the fourth plate. The cat ignored it, opened its mouth, and mewed a second time.

This time Till swiveled on his chair. "Somewhere . . . I don't know from which direction . . . but there's something— very faint—like, oh, I don't know what . . ." He dared not say aloud what he was thinking.

"Meow!"

Low-voiced, old Miss Gammer said, *"Thrice the brinded cat hath mewed."* Then, listening intently, she muttered, *"'Tis time—'tis time!"* Before she had finished speaking, the cat had gone. It had flashed from its chair back to old Miss Gammer's cottage; they heard the rattle of the cat flap as the kitty rushed through.

And now, out of the blue, they could hear the unmistakable sound of a dog barking, distant and faint at first, but very swiftly coming nearer—growing louder . . . nearer.

"It's Bess!" shouted Till, and sprang to his feet. It was well for the others that his springing up took him away from the tea table, for the little dog that came at him out of nowhere knocked him over with the force of her arrival. As it was, in the joyful muddling of boy and dog on the ground, a corner of the tablecloth was tweaked, so that the teapot was overset, the figure of Mudman flew into a flower bed, and the jam spoon whisked off somewhere and was not found until a week later. Miss Mousy was trying to stop all these things from happening, and old Miss Gammer was trying to help her—but laughing too much to be very useful.

And on the ground the boy and the dog were tangling together—the dog slapping her tongue over the boy's face while she danced and pranced on his body as he tried to clutch and clasp her to him, to grab and grasp and grip her.

And suddenly she had to be free—free—and she tore herself away from him and was racing at top speed right around the meadow, barking at the top of her voice, so that in a great flurry the ducks flew from the riverbank into the river, the squirrels peered down from their treetops, and a distant heron rose wearily into the air and departed.

Till, almost breathless but on his feet again, was watching the little dog as she ran and ran. He said, "Now do you see why I call her Bess?"

"Short for Elizabeth?" said old Miss Gammer.

"That's what everybody thinks," said Till. "But they're wrong. That's just her ordinary name. My secret name for her—her real name—is hidden in her ordinary name, and it's short for something quite different. It's spelled with one *s*, not two: *B-e-s*—Bes. You can try guessing—"

He broke off to admire his dog in the grace and speed of her distant running. Now she had paused among the molehills to sniff at one that had been tampered with. It interested her; she dug at it for a while.

Miss Mousy said, "Is her secret name Besom, like a witch's broom?"

"No," said Till.

"There's not much choice, then," said old Miss Gammer. "Beseem—Bespoke—Besought—Besprinkled —Bespangled—Bespattered—"

"No—no—no—no—no—no!" Till was laughing at the absurd names suggested. "Do you give up?"

"Certainly not. How many letters in this secret name?"

"That's as good as telling. But here's a clue. There are six words in the whole answer, and the first word—the *Bes* word—is shorter than all the possible words you've thought of so far."

Miss Mousy said, "Even shorter than Besom? It can't be!"

"It is."

And now Bess was suddenly among them again at full tilt and then off again around the meadow, and this time Till went racing after her, calling back over his shoulder as he went, "Her secret name is Best-in-the-Whole-Wide-World!"

Later, quite tired out at last, Till sat down to tea. He ate six scones straight off, with raspberry jam and cream. Bess had smelled something interesting in the flower bed and found her old bedtime toy, Mudman. So she was allowed to sit on the fourth chair, mumbling Mudman between her teeth.

Looking at her on the fourth chair, Till said, "Do you think he had to fight his brother to get her back for me?"

"I doubt it," said old Miss Gammer. "Remember, he had that magnificent new collar you gave him. That would be better than any battle-ax in an argument."

"So nobody was killed?"

"Good gracious, no!"

Till nodded and took his last scone. "I wish I could have thanked him."

After tea, Till and Bess went for a swing on the tire.

And after that they would go home together, taking Mudman with them.

Miss Mousy had made a fresh pot of tea, and she and old Miss Gammer sat sipping their tea and watching Till on the swing—*up and down, up and down*—with Bess running alongside it, trying to catch a loose end of rope as it flew past with the swinging.

Old Miss Gammer sighed. She said, "It would make such a good story."

Miss Mousy said, "Why don't you do it, then?"

"You mean, write it?"

"Why not? Till could help you remember things. And I could do the pictures. I'd like to do one of Till on the swing with his Bess. Just as now."

Old Miss Gammer thought. "I could start the story: 'Once upon a time . . .'"

"No, no! That makes it sound like a fairy story, but everything really did happen. Here. Today."

"So perhaps I should just begin: 'There was a boy . . .'"

"That's it. And the very end of your story can be my

picture of the cream tea party—or the boy and his dog together again."

Old Miss Gammer said, "I think the writer should have the last word, or words."

Miss Mousy said, "Oh?" Then, "What are these last special words?"

"Only two," said Miss Gammer.

"THE END."

∾

First U.S. edition 2009

Library of Congress Cataloging-in-Publication Data

Pearce, Philippa.

A finder's magic / Philippa Pearce ; illustrated by Helen Craig. —1st U.S. ed.

p.   cm.

Summary: After a mysterious stranger offers to help Till find his dog, they embark on
a magical quest, interviewing various witnesses including a heron, a mole, a riddling cat,
and Miss Mousey, whose sketch of a peaceful riverbank offers a vital clue.

ISBN 978-0-7636-4072-9

[1. Lost and found possessions—Fiction. 2. Magic—Fiction.]

I. Title. II. Craig, Helen, ill.

PZ7.P3145 Fi 2009

[Fic]—dc22   2008017533

2 4 6 8 10 9 7 5 3 1

Printed in China

This book was typeset in Poliphilus MT.
The illustrations were done in TK.

Candlewick Press
99 Dover Street
Somerville, Massachusetts 02144

visit us at www.candlewick.com